Tools for Toys

By Marcy Kelman
Illustrated by Alan Batson
Based on the episode written by Michael Maurer

NEW YORK

An Imprint of Disney Book Group

DISNEP PRESS

First Edition 10 9 8 7 6 5 4 3 2 1
Library of Congress Cataloging-in-Publication Data on file
ISBN 978-1-4231-1029-3

Manufactured in the USA
For more Disney Press fun, visit www.disneybooks.com

"Argh—this last screw sure is tight!" groaned Turner, as he struggled to turn a screw on a vacuum cleaner that the team needed to repair. "It's…just…not…turning."

Eager to help, Squeeze grabbed hold of Turner's head. "I'll help you unscrew it, Turner!"

"Ow—you're squeezing too hard," grunted Turner. "I'm getting a headache!"

"Easy does it, Squeeze," cautioned Manny.

"I'll help," Stretch offered, wrapping his tape measure around Squeeze.

Turner, Squeeze, and Stretch pulled and tugged with all their might.

"It's turning! It's turning!" cried Rusty.

Pat was getting anxious. "It probably just needs one good tap to come loose!" He jumped up and tapped Squeeze. As the screw whirled out of the vacuum cleaner, all of the tools swiveled along with it before crashing down with a *thud*!

Manny made sure the tools were okay. "Hmm…maybe we should take a little break?" he suggested.

"Break? Huh? D-d-did something break?" Rusty worried.

"No, nothing's broken, Rusty," explained Stretch. "Manny means a rest. Sometimes it's good to take a step back from work and clear your head. Taking breaks from work is important."

"Oh, phooey, I'm not taking a break," grumbled Turner. "Let's get this job done!"

Pat agreed with Turner. "Yeah, let's finish the job!" In his excitement, Pat jumped up and accidentally landed on the vacuum's power switch.

VA-ROOOOOOOM!

The vacuum's hose sprung into action, twisting like a snake. Suddenly, Turner was sucked up into the hose!

Pat gulped. "Oops! Maybe taking a break wasn't such a bad idea after all."

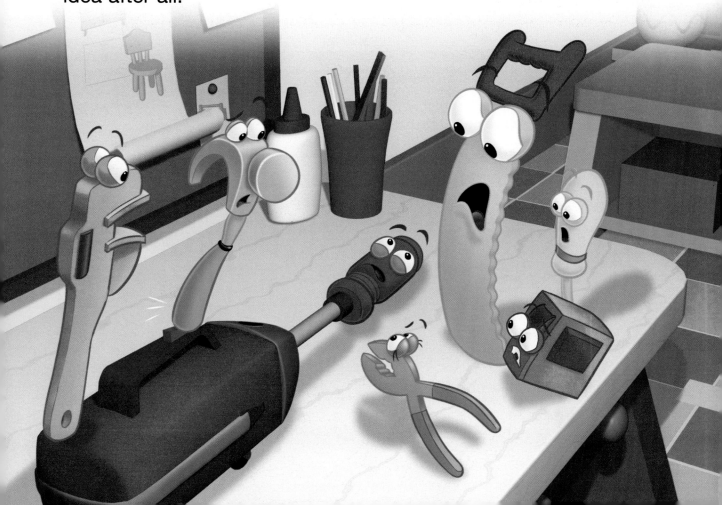

Manny switched off the vacuum. "*¿Estás bien?* You okay, Turner?"

Turner crawled out of the vacuum hose, coughing and sneezing.

"You see, Turner? It's not healthy to get sucked into your work!" laughed Felipe.

"Aww, gimme a break!" snarled Turner.

Squeeze cheered. "That's the spirit, Turner! Taking a break will make you feel better."

Turner was getting frustrated. "*Grrrrr*, let's put the brakes on all this break talk, shall we?"

Dusty started to giggle. "Hey, you know what they say—breaking up is hard to do!"

"That's it!" yelled Turner. "If I hear the word 'break' again, I swear I'll—"

Just then, Manny's phone rang.

"*Hola*, Handy Manny's Repair Shop. You—" Manny paused for a second and smiled at Turner. "Uh, you damage it, we fix it!"

Turner rolled his eyes and muttered under his breath.

"Manny? This is Mr. Singh," said the voice on the other end of the telephone.

"Hello, Mr. Singh," Manny greeted him. "Can we help you?"

"I hope so. I've been so busy with work lately, and I have quite a few things around the house that I just haven't had time to fix myself," explained Mr. Singh.

Look around Mr. Singh's yard. Can you spot three things that need to be repaired?

"What do you need us to repair, Mr. Singh?" asked Manny.

"Well, my daughter's swing set has a broken bolt, her doll carriage has a wobbly wheel, and we have a picnic bench with a few loose boards," explained Mr. Singh. "My to-do list just keeps growing, but it seems I can never find the time to do these things. I'm always working!"

"*Si*, we know what that's like," said Manny. "Don't worry, Mr. Singh, we'll be right over!"

Mr. Singh was relieved. "Oh, that's great. Thank you, Manny!"

On their way to Mr. Singh's house, Manny and the tools saw Mr. Lopart fiddling with a CD player outside his candy shop.

"*Hola*, Mr. Lopart. *¿Que pasa?* What's happening?"

"Oh, hello, Manny. I was just about to play my new theme song for my candy store. I wrote it myself! It's what the kids call 'hip'!"

"Well, we'd love to hear it, Mr. Lopart," smiled Manny.

Mr. Lopart turned on the CD player, and a hip-hop beat started to play. Mr. Lopart began to move and groove to the music.

To everyone's surprise, Mr. Lopart started rapping. "I am the Candy Wrapper. Lopart is my name. I sell lollipops, jelly beans, and candy canes! I've got fireballs, licorice, bubble gum, and more. So when you need something sweet, come on down to my stoooooooooore!"

Mr. Lopart accidentally bumped into the CD player, causing an ear-splitting sound.

Manny ran over to turn down the volume. "There must be something wrong with the speakers. Want me to take a look at it?"

"Oh, that's okay, I can handle it myself," Mr. Lopart assured him.

Once Manny and the tools left for Mr. Singh's house, Mr. Lopart started banging on the CD player. Instantly, the music sped up, and the volume got higher and higher until—*CRASH!* Mr. Lopart's storefront window shattered from the high-pitched noise!

Mr. Lopart laughed nervously. "Uh, now that's what I call a breakthrough hit, Fluffy!"

At Mr. Singh's house, Manny and the tools inspected the swing set that needed to be repaired.

"I think I have the right-size bolt in my truck, Mr. Singh," Manny said.

"Great, Manny," said Mr. Singh.

"Daddy! Daddy!" shouted a little girl, pushing her wobbly doll carriage toward Mr. Singh.

"Hello, Leela," smiled Mr. Singh. "This is Manny. He's come with his tools to fix your swings."

Leela was thrilled. "Goody! That means we can play on them right after the tea party with my dollies. Right, Daddy?"

"Uh…tea party?" said Mr. Singh, looking at his watch. "Well, I would love to, sweetheart…but I'm expecting a phone call any minute. I have a very busy day."

Leela's smile disappeared. She was sad to hear this.

"Don't worry, Leela, we will have that tea party very soon," promised Mr. Singh.

"Okay, Daddy," Leela murmured, looking down with disappointment.

While Manny and Stretch went to inspect the broken picnic bench with Mr. Singh, the rest of the tools got ready to work on Leela's doll carriage.

"Hi, Mister Tool!" Leela exclaimed to Turner.

"Er...yeah...hi—hey!" shouted Turner, as Leela picked him up. "What are you doing with me?"

"Would you like to play with me?" Leela asked sweetly.

"Uh, sorry, I-I-I can't do that. I-I-I'm a tool, n-n-not a toy…" Turner stammered.

Felipe chuckled. "Ha! *Si*, Turner is definitely not a toy. In fact, he isn't even *fun*!"

"Aw, you're cute, Tooly!" gushed Leela. "I think you'd make a really nice dolly. Are you hungry?"

Before Turner could answer, Leela put a toy baby bottle in Turner's mouth.

The tools started to giggle.

When they finally stopped laughing, the tools realized that Leela had wheeled Turner away in her doll carriage. They had to rescue him.

"Uh, excuse me, little girl," said Rusty, who found Leela playing with her dollhouse. "We've come to get our friend, Turner."

"Oh, you mean my dolly," exclaimed Leela. "Tooly! Come out! Your friends are here."

"No! I can't!" shrieked Turner from inside the dollhouse.

"Ohh, *por que* no? Why not?" teased Felipe. "Are you playing hide-and-seek, Drooly—er, I mean, Tooly?"

Embarrassed, Turner peeked through the dollhouse window wearing a pink doll bonnet. The tools howled with laughter.

"Wow, you look absolutely toy-riffic," Dusty guffawed.

"Okay, Turner, playtime is over," joked Felipe. "We have work to do!"

"Aw, but we were having so much fun. Can't you stay and have tea and pie with us? Oh, please?" begged Leela.

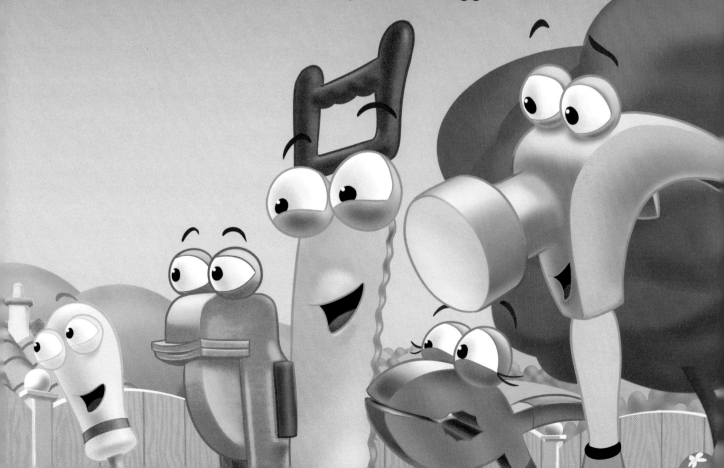

"But we have a squeaky wheel to fix," reasoned Squeeze. "Maybe we should play after we're done."

"That's right. Sorry, kid, but we gotta go!" Turner sighed with relief.

Leela frowned. "My dad never has time for tea and pie either. He always says he's very busy, too."

Dusty felt bad. "Gosh, I don't think we're too busy for a little tea party. Isn't that right, Turner?"

"Aw, I guess not," Turner finally said, and he and the tools made mud pies and drank make-believe tea with Leela.

Before long, Manny, Stretch, and Mr. Singh checked in on the tools. Manny hoped that the doll carriage had already been fixed.

Manny was surprised. "What's going on here?"

"Um, we took a little tea break to play with Leela," confessed Dusty.

"Well, taking a short break is fine," Manny began, "but now it's time for my tools to get back to work, Leela."

Leela gave Turner a kiss before handing him over to Manny.
"You can go, Tooly," Leela whimpered. "You don't have to play with me."
Seeing his daughter so sad made Mr. Singh feel awful.
"Oh, don't worry—I'll play with you, Leela."
"B-b-but, you're too busy, Daddy," cried Leela.

"Too busy? Is that what you think, sweetie?" Mr. Singh hugged his daughter. Just then, Mr. Singh's phone rang. Instead of answering it, he shut it off. "I can't think of anything more important than spending special time with you, Leela. So how about a nice cup of tea?"

"And some mud pie?" Leela asked hopefully.

"Of course, it's my favorite!" laughed Mr. Singh.

As Mr. Singh and Leela went off to play, Manny and the tools got to work on their repairs.

When Manny and the tools finished their work, they said good-bye to Mr. Singh and Leela, who were still playing with the dollhouse.

"Thanks for all of your hard work—and play!" Mr. Singh said to Manny and the tools.

Manny grinned. "Our pleasure, Mr. Singh."

"Bye, Tooly! Here's a little gift for you," Leela said as she tied the pink bonnet on Turner.

"You know, Turner, you look pretty good when you're all *dolled up*!" teased Felipe.

"Ack, when will he stop toying with me?" Turner groaned. Everyone laughed.